Flower Girls #1

Violet

The Flower Girls #1
Violet

by Kathleen Leverich
Illustrated by Lynne Woodcock Cravath

HarperTrophy®
A Division of HarperCollinsPublishers

Library of Congress Cataloging-in-Publication Data
Leverich, Kathleen
Violet / by Kathleen Leverich ; illustrated by Lynne Woodcock Cravath.
    p.   cm. — (Flower Girls ; #1)
Summary: Shy, proper Violet is asked to be a flower girl in her cousin's punk wedding and must decide
whether she wants to or not.
    ISBN 0-06-442018-3 (pbk.)
    [1. Weddings—Fiction.   2. Individuality—Fiction.]   I. Cravath, Lynne Woodcock, ill.   II. Title.
III. Series: Leverich, Kathleen.   Flower Girls ; #1.
PZ7.L5744Vi 1997   96-111
[Fic]—dc20   CIP
                                                                                                            AC

4   5   6   7   8   9   10
❖
First Edition

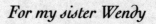

For my sister Wendy

Chapter 1

Violet Wing had a secret.

It thrilled her to the soles of her neatly shined shoes.

It also worried her.

That was no surprise. Most things worried eight-year-old Violet.

Speaking up in school worried her. What if she gave the wrong answer?

Playing softball worried her. What if she dropped the ball?

Violet stole a glance at the three girls sitting on the bench with her. She took a deep breath. She never kept secrets from Rose, Heather, and Daisy. They were her best friends.

"Look!" said Heather.

"There's the first car!" Daisy pointed to the far side of the pond.

Rose pulled Daisy's arm down. "Don't point. It's impolite."

It was the first Saturday in April.

Violet and her friends were sitting on their usual bench in Pleasant Park. It was the Flower Girl bench, named for their club: the Flower Girls.

The club had been Rose's idea. Each of the four members had a flower name. Each wanted to be a real flower girl in a wedding.

Every weekend they met here, in the park. It was the best place in town to see weddings.

"Here they come!" cried Daisy.

Rose and Heather leaned forward to watch.

Violet leaned forward too.

 2

Every couple in town came to Pleasant Park to have their wedding photos taken.

In spring the bridal parties would stand beside the tulips. In summer they posed in the shade of the Japanese tea-house. In autumn they stood under maples ablaze with red and gold leaves. Winter bridal parties rode through the snow in horse-drawn sleighs.

Violet liked spring weddings best. She watched now as six bridesmaids in lavender gowns stepped out of two limousines. Six ushers followed them onto the grass.

A third limo pulled up. Out of it stepped the groom. He reached back into the limo and offered his hand. . . .

"There she is!" cried Daisy.

"Where?" said Heather.

Rose said, "There! Violet, do you see?"

Violet saw.

She wasn't the bride. *She* was Kara Cassidy, a first grader. Kara wore a long, filmy dress and a wreath of flowers in her hair.

She was the flower girl.

"When I'm a flower girl, I'll wear a long gown," said Daisy.

"When I'm a flower girl, I'll carry lilies-of-the-valley," said Rose.

Heather said, "If someone doesn't ask us soon, it'll be too late. We'll be too old to be flower girls!"

I should tell my secret right now, thought Violet.

She smoothed the skirt of her starched dress. She smoothed her chin-length black hair that never needed smoothing.

The sooner I speak up, the better, thought Violet.

But Violet didn't speak up. Violet never spoke up. Violet listened. Violet watched. Violet was shy.

The bridesmaids spread the bride's long train on the grass.

"I'll have a train when I get married," said Rose. She was tall, thin, and delicate-looking. She had long red hair and the palest skin. "I want my wedding to be just like this."

Heather turned to stare at her. "Like this? You're kidding! The bridesmaids' dresses are too short. The bride's gown is too fussy. Lavender as a wedding color went out of style last year. . . ."

Heather was the shortest of the Flower Girls, and the sturdiest. She was also the youngest. She had skipped first grade and was only seven and a half years old.

Heather was smart and funny, but she

was an awful snob. She found something wrong with every wedding the Flower Girls saw.

"Besides," said Heather, "six brides-maids are too many. A bride should have at least one attendant but fewer than five."

"I've never heard that rule," said Daisy.

"Who decided that?" said Rose.

Heather shrugged. "It's a well-known bridal fact. No wedding I'm in will have more than four attendants. This wedding has too many. That shows terrible taste."

"Quiet!" Rose hushed her. "The bride and groom will hear you."

Heather tossed her head. Her huge cloud of crinkly, honey-colored hair bounced. She folded her arms. "Let them hear. What do I care? It's the truth."

Unlike Violet, Heather never worried about hurting people's feelings. She couldn't care less what people thought of her.

Violet wished she could toss her head and fold her arms the way Heather did. She wished she could say whatever was on her mind. Her secret, for instance.

"Which usher do you like the best?" asked Daisy.

Daisy was the prettiest Flower Girl. The others all agreed. She had dark brown skin, dark brown eyes, and complicated hair. Every six weeks a hairdresser wove Daisy's hair into five hundred neat, chin-length braids.

Exactly five hundred.

Heather had counted once, just to see.

Daisy dressed in pastel frills, but she could run faster than anyone in the third grade—boys included. She could toss a football farther. She was the most popular girl in the third grade.

Violet looked at the ushers who stood around the groom.

One usher smacked the groom's shoulder.

Three others doubled over, laughing.

"I like the one with the beard," said Rose.

Heather rolled her eyes. "You like *beards*?"

The fifth picked a speck of lint off the sixth's tuxedo jacket.

None is as handsome as the groom, thought Violet.

As she watched, the groom caught Kara Cassidy by the waist. He lifted her and twirled her in the air. Kara gripped the groom's shoulders. Her filmy dress billowed in the breeze. Her laughter pealed out over the park. . . .

Violet imagined just what Kara was feeling. She imagined herself in a long, filmy dress being twirled over the grass. . . .

"What a show-off that Kara is!" said Heather.

Violet blinked. "Show-off? How is she showing off?"

Daisy nudged Violet. "Want to know why Heather is grouchy?"

Heather scowled at Daisy. "You don't know my reasons. You're not a mind reader."

Daisy whispered to Violet, "Heather is jealous!"

Heather leaped to her feet and glowered at Daisy. "Me? Jealous of Kara Cassidy?"

Heather criticized other people all the

time. But she couldn't stand to have anyone criticize her.

Violet knew that. So did Rose. But only Daisy knew how to tease Heather about it.

"Take that back!" Heather stamped a foot.

Daisy grinned at Violet.

Violet couldn't help but grin back.

Violet wished she could act as carefree as Daisy. She wished she could whisper in that just-loud-enough voice that made one person scowl and everyone else laugh.

"Kara isn't showing off," said Daisy. "She's enjoying herself."

"I say she's a show-off!" said Heather. "I'd make a better flower girl than her. I'd make a better flower girl than you."

"Stop it, both of you!" Rose's face was

 12

flushed. Her fists were clenched. She was so angry that when she shut her eyes, the lids fluttered.

Violet was glad Rose wasn't angry at her.

Rose might look delicate. She might look fragile. But Rose had definite ideas about what was right and what was wrong. She stood for no nonsense.

When Rose gave an order, everyone obeyed.

Rose tucked a stray lock of red hair under her wide-brimmed straw hat. "We'd all make good flower girls. That's why we're in this club. Stop arguing about it. You're acting immature."

Daisy rolled her eyes.

Heather tossed her head.

But they quieted down.

Violet wished she had a stray lock of

hair to tuck behind her ear. She wished she could clench her fists and flutter her eyelids in the grown-up way Rose did.

Rose gazed across the pond at the bridal party. "We *have* to be flower girls. With names like ours, it's only right."

Daisy arched her back and stretched. "We will be flower girls. I want us to be flower girls."

"Your *wanting* us to be flower girls hasn't helped anyone so far." Heather tossed her head. She folded her arms. "None of us has even been asked."

Violet chewed her lip. She could tell them now.

"What's wrong with you, Violet?"

Violet blinked.

Rose was staring at her.

"You're shaking like a leaf." Daisy stared too.

 14

Heather narrowed her eyes. "Are you keeping something from us, Violet?"

Violet kept her eyes on the gravel path. "I wasn't keeping it from you. I only found out this morning. I was going to tell you. . . ."

"Spit it out!" said Heather.

Violet swallowed hard. "I'm going to be a flower girl."

Chapter 2

"All right, Violet!" said Rose.

"It's about time one of us was asked!" Daisy grinned.

Heather said, "I'm glad you're first. You'll set a good example. Any wedding you're in will be in perfect taste. Your mother will make sure."

Violet's hands stopped sweating. The knot in her stomach loosened up.

"Where will the wedding be?" asked Rose.

"When?" asked Daisy.

Heather lassoed her hair with a barrette. "Who are the bride and groom?"

Violet said, "The wedding will be right here in town."

"Good!" said Rose.

"We'll be able to see it!" Daisy clapped her hands.

Violet started to feel excited. Her friends didn't mind. Everything was all right. "The wedding date is April twenty-seventh."

Heather frowned. "April twenty-seventh, *this* year?"

Violet nodded.

Heather stared. "That's just three weeks from today."

"Never mind that," said Rose. "Tell us the rest. What will you wear?"

"Something perfect," said Daisy.

"Everything Violet owns is perfect," said Heather. "Violet's mother only buys perfect stuff."

Violet's mother chose all Violet's dresses.

She chose Violet's hairstyle and her shoes and socks too.

Violet's mother had excellent taste. Even Heather said so.

Violet said, "My mother wants us to find a one-of-a-kind dress. We're going to the city tomorrow to look."

"The city?" said Daisy.

"That's good," said Rose. "There are more bridal shops in the city than out here. They have a bigger selection of dresses."

Heather nodded. "I'll bet your mother takes you to Sugar 'n' Spice. Their clothes are the fanciest."

"Their clothes are the most expensive!" said Rose.

Rose's mother was divorced. She worked as a nurse at the hospital. Violet's mother said Mrs. Noble and Rose had enough money to be comfortable, but they had to be careful. They couldn't afford to buy extras.

Violet sometimes felt guilty about that. She had two parents who could buy her anything she wanted. She never had to think about how much things cost.

Violet said, "I don't know if we'll go to Sugar 'n' Spice. My cousin might have other plans."

"Cousin? Which cousin?" asked Heather.

"The one who grew up here in town," said Violet. "Roxy. Roxy Chew."

Heather frowned. "I remember Roxy. My big brother and his friends went to high school with her. They called her Foxy Roxy. Her mother has been married a million times."

"Roxy worked after school in my parents' store," said Daisy. "She always got

there late because she always had deten-
tion. But once she was there, Roxy could
sell anyone anything."

"Roxy knows how to wrap people
around her little finger," agreed Rose.
"Does she still ride a motorcycle, Violet?
Does she still get into trouble? Does her
hair still reach her waist?"

Violet shrugged. "Roxy plays drums
in a band now. She's been on tour. I
haven't seen her in a year."

Heather tossed a pebble in the pond.
"Imagine! You're going to be Foxy
Roxy's flower girl."

Violet nodded. "She called last night.
Her mother's away. She wants my mom
to help her with the wedding."

"Who's the groom?" asked Daisy.

"Roxy's boyfriend," said Violet. "Zoot."

Daisy looked startled.

Rose frowned. "What kind of a name is that?"

Violet shrugged. "He has a store in the city. It sells . . . I don't know what it sells. It's downtown. That's where we're meeting Roxy tomorrow."

Heather gasped. "You're not shopping for a dress downtown, are you?"

"I don't think so," said Violet.

Heather folded her arms and tossed her head. "I should hope not! Downtown bridal shops sell the worst clothes."

Violet turned to Daisy and Rose. "Is that true?"

Rose shrugged.

"Heather's the expert," said Daisy.

"That's right," said Heather. "And I say you have a problem. Roxy can't arrange a wedding in three weeks. Where will she find a band? What about a caterer? What about a place for the reception? A proper wedding gets planned months in advance."

"A 'proper' wedding is the last kind of wedding Roxy would want," said Rose.

Daisy nodded. "Roxy's not the proper type. She's wild."

Violet tried to stay calm. "She's not

wild. Roxy's unusual. That's what my mother says."

"I smell disaster." Heather folded her arms.

"Disaster?" Violet started to tremble.

Rose nudged Heather. "Cut it out! You're upsetting Violet."

"Violet's mother will make sure Roxy's wedding is nice. She'll make sure it's perfect," said Daisy.

"That's right," said Rose.

Violet wanted to believe Daisy and Rose.

She was sure her mother would do her best, but . . .

Violet remembered the night three years earlier when Roxy came to baby-sit. No sooner did Violet's parents leave the house than Roxy's friends began to arrive. Fifty of them. They blasted music on the

stereo. They phoned for take-out pizza, ribs, and Mexican food. They got into the hot tub with their clothes on. They treated Violet as if she were a big kid and let her stay up late. At five minutes to midnight they cleaned up everything and left.

"Let's not tell your parents about this," Roxy had said. Violet hadn't told . . . but the neighbors had.

"Disaster," said Heather.

Violet was afraid Heather might be right.

Chapter 3

The next day Violet drove with her mother into the city.

The day was warm, but Violet's mother looked cool in her crisp tan suit, brown-and-white high heels, and white blouse. The pearls around her neck glowed. Her black hair was fastened in a perfect French twist.

Violet buckled her seat belt and settled back in the seat.

Her mother drove the car through the traffic on the highway. She speeded up. She slowed down. She paid tolls.

Violet wondered, *Will I ever be grown-up and calm like Mom? Will I ever do things perfectly?*

Violet's mother glanced at her and frowned. "Don't bite your nails, sweetheart."

Violet stopped biting. She folded her hands in her lap. "Perfect" was something she never would be.

Violet's mother found a parking space right in front of Zoot's shop.

While her mother dropped quarters in the parking meter, Violet stood on the sidewalk. She smoothed her blouse. She straightened her socks.

"Hey, Little Bo Peep!"

Violet glanced up.

A tough kid grinned at her from the opposite side of the street. He was nine or ten. His skin was light brown. His hair was short. He wore baggy shorts and a black T-shirt. He glided down the sidewalk on a skateboard.

"Want to try my board?"

The kid glided back and forth on the sidewalk. He grinned at Violet. "My name's Andre. What's yours?"

Violet took a step closer to her mother.

The kid burst out laughing, turned on the board, and zoomed off.

Violet shivered.

She was glad she didn't live in the city. She'd have to go to school with that scary kid.

She stood on her toes to peer after him. He certainly rode that skateboard well....

"Let's hurry, Violet." Violet's mother dropped the car keys in her purse and turned toward the shop.

Violet hurried after her mother.

TRASH TREASURES said the sign above the shop door. Smaller letters underneath said PRE-OWNED CLOTHES.

The shop was dimly lit and stuffy.

A narrow aisle led from the front door to a counter.

Clothes racks stood on either side. They bulged with musty-smelling clothes.

Handmade signs hung on the walls. Others were posted on the counter.

"BODY PIERCING DONE NOW!"

"TATTOOS. YOUR DESIGNS OR OURS."

"SALE!!! ALL FACE JEWELRY 15% OFF."

A girl wearing dark glasses sat behind the counter. She glanced up as Violet and her mother entered.

Violet didn't mean to gasp. But she had never seen a girl with a buzz cut. Or a girl with a diamond stud in her nose.

Violet's mother said, "Excuse me, uh, young lady. . . ? We're looking for Miss Chew. Roxanne Chew?"

29

The girl grinned.

She came out from behind the counter.

Violet couldn't help but notice the spiked leather bracelets the girl wore up and down both arms.

She couldn't help but stare at the butterfly tattoo on the outside of the girl's left knee.

The girl saw Violet staring. She tapped the heel of her heavy black work-boot on the floor. As her knee bent and straightened, the butterfly seemed to flutter around it.

The girl grinned at Violet.

Violet forgot the shaved head and the butterfly tattoo. She recognized that grin. "Roxy?"

The girl yanked off her dark glasses. She flung her arms wide. "The one and only!"

Chapter 4

Roxy gave Violet's mother a big kiss. "Aunt Liz!"

She hugged Violet and stood back to look at her. "You've grown up!"

Violet blushed with pleasure.

Roxy let go of Violet's shoulders. "Well, flower girl, let's pick something for you to wear."

Violet's mother smiled. "Sugar 'n' Spice has perfect flower girl dresses. We thought we'd look for a pale pink gown with puffed sleeves and a full skirt."

Violet turned to Roxy. "Would that be all right?"

"Puffed sleeves? Pale pink?" Roxy stuck a finger in her mouth and pretended to gag. "You need a dress that's trashy."

Violet blinked.

Violet's mother fingered her pearls. "*Trashy?* I'm afraid I don't understand."

Roxy leaned against the counter.

Her miniskirt rode up her thighs.

She tapped a foot.

The butterfly on her knee fluttered.

She said, "I'm going to have a punk wedding. It'll be part wedding, part joke."

"Joke?" Violet's mother's voice sounded faint. "You want to treat your wedding as a joke?"

Roxy's eyes grew wide and imploring. "I know exactly what I want, Aunt Liz. It's my wedding. Please go along. . . ."

Violet remembered what Daisy had said. *Roxy could sell anyone anything. . . .*

Roxy stepped close to Violet's mother.

"Pleeease? I've been counting on your support."

Violet's mother hesitated. But then she smiled and put an arm around Roxy's shoulders. "I'll support you, dear, of course. But what does Father Driscoll say? I can't see him having a punk wedding at Our Lady of Flowers."

"Neither can Father Driscoll!" Roxy grinned and stepped away. She glanced in a display mirror to check her mascara. "That's why we're having the ceremony at Oil City instead. You know, 'Thirty pumps. Thirty!' It's the giant gas station just outside town."

"A service station?" Violet's mother stared.

Violet stared too. Nothing was happening the way she'd expected.

Roxy said, "Father Driscoll didn't

approve, so we asked our neighborhood priest, Father Jake, to come. Most Saturdays he marries inmates at the city jail. But that Saturday he'll marry us at Oil City. As a special favor."

Violet's mother passed a hand across her eyes. "Roxanne, you're your mother all over again."

Violet shivered.

Roxy's mother was Aunt Glenda. Aunt Glenda was Violet's mother's older sister. Her *scary* older sister. That's what Violet's father always said.

"Where is Glenda . . . your mother, now? Does anyone know?" asked Violet's mother.

Roxy nodded. "Glenda's in Brazil, in the rain forest. She's hunting for medicinal plants with her new husband."

"Bertrand?" said Violet's mother.

"Bertrand is history. Glenda's married to Joao now. He's an Indian healer. He's her fifth." Roxy ran a hand over her buzz cut.

Violet wondered, *How would I look with short spiky hair?*

How would it feel to have a butterfly fluttering on my knee?

Would skintight clothes feel comfortable?

"Shouldn't we get in touch with your mother? She could help. She's had . . ." Violet's mother searched for the right words. "She's had so much experience with weddings."

Roxy shrugged. "I've had experience too. I've been going to Glenda's weddings since I was Violet's age. Besides, there's nothing left to help with. Everything is set."

Violet's mother cocked her head. "What about cars? You'll need to rent limousines."

Roxy rolled her eyes. "Limos are corny, Aunt Liz. We're renting wrecks from Hire-a-Heap."

Violet's mother flinched. She tried again. "What about the reception? It's short notice, but there's the country club."

"We've hired a hall," said Roxy.

Violet's mother looked hopeful. "Which one? Ten Oaks Manor? We've been to some lovely receptions at Ten Oaks."

"Not Ten Oaks," said Roxy. "Fast Lanes."

Violet's mother frowned. "I beg your pardon?"

"Fast Lanes," said Violet. "The bowling alley."

Violet had never been to Fast Lanes. Some of her friends had bowled there, but Violet hadn't been allowed to. She had always wondered about Fast Lanes.

Roxy went on. "We can walk there from Oil City instead of driving. That's a plus. The Hire-a-Heap cars are more for looks than transportation."

"Have you thought about caterers? And what about music? You'll need a band," said Violet's mother.

Roxy stretched. "I have a band, Aunt Lizzy. I'm a band *leader*. Besides, Fast Lanes has a giant juke box."

Violet thought her mother looked ready to give up.

"And food?"

"The Fast Lanes snack bar will take care of that. They'll serve hot dogs, popcorn, and slushes. They're going to construct a wedding cake out of snack cakes."

Violet looked at her mother.

Violet's mother didn't allow snack cakes in their house.

Roxy said, "Do you think they should take the plastic wrappers off the cakes when they stack them? Or leave them on?"

Violet's mother winced.

Violet thought, *If they're wedding cake, Mom will have to let me eat at least one. . . .*

Roxy turned to Violet. "Let's see what we'll dress you in, flower girl."

Violet snapped to attention.

"Fake fur?" Roxy pulled a leopard-skin jumpsuit off a rack.

"Vinyl?" Roxy selected a pink vinyl dress with a white vinyl coat. "You said you liked pink."

Violet's mother shook her head.

"How about mohair?" Roxy held up an orange mohair miniskirt with a lavender mohair crop top.

Violet looked from one outfit to another.

Roxy said, "I like the leopard skin, but I'm the 'wild animal' type. Which type are you?"

Violet's eyes went straight to the orange miniskirt and lavender top. That outfit was loud, rude, and completely unladylike.

Violet pointed.

"Great!" said Roxy. "That's what you'll wear."

"I couldn't!" said Violet. She remembered what Heather had said about the lavender bridesmaids' dresses. "Besides, lavender as a wedding color went out of style last year."

"Even better!" Roxy grinned. She held the outfit up to Violet.

Violet's mother cleared her throat. She drew Violet to her. "Roxanne, thank you for showing us these interesting outfits. Violet and I will think them over and let you know."

She ushered Violet out the shop door.

Once on the sidewalk Violet's mother mopped her brow. She straightened her skirt. "If Roxanne would only grow her hair, take out that awful diamond stud, and put on a nice dress, she'd look just fine. She has such a pretty face."

Violet tried to imagine Roxy that way.

It was as hard as trying to imagine her mother dressed in a leopard-skin jumpsuit.

Her mother took out the car keys. "Let's drive straight to Sugar 'n' Spice. We'll find a pale pink dress with a full skirt and puffed sleeves. We'll buy it. You'll wear it. That will be that."

Violet followed her mother across the sidewalk to the car. She felt relieved. She'd have the perfect flower girl dress. Her mother would somehow talk Roxy into having a wedding that was perfect too.

"Hey, Bo Peep!"

42

Violet turned.

The skateboarder, Andre, was gliding by across the street. "Come ride my board!"

Violet swallowed hard. She hurried

after her mother. She wouldn't feel safe until they'd climbed into their car and locked the doors.

"So long, Bo Peep. See you in three weeks."

Violet stopped short.

Three weeks?

She turned to face Andre.

He held up three fingers. He wiggled them. "Roxy's my friend. So is Zoot. They've asked me to be in their wedding."

As what? Violet wondered.

"I'll be ring bearer. At the reception, you and I will be partners."

"Come along, Violet!" called Violet's mother.

Andre slalomed away.

Violet wiped her palms. They had started to sweat.

Chapter 5

Violet and her mother drove to Sugar 'n' Spice. They found the perfect pale pink flower girl dress. They bought it and drove home.

The following Friday after school, Violet met the other Flower Girls in the park.

Violet told them about the dress.

Then she told them everything else.

"*Oil City?*" said Rose.

"*Fast Lanes?*" said Daisy.

Heather folded her arms and tossed her head. "Disaster! I knew it."

Violet nodded. "Roxy is coming out here this afternoon. She'll spend the night at our house. Tomorrow she'll make wedding arrangements. We're looking for the perfect place to pick dandelions for my bouquet."

"You can't carry dandelions!" said Heather.

"It's mean of Roxy to ask you!" said Rose.

"Roxy isn't mean," said Violet. "She's unusual. She wants her wedding to be unusual too."

"I've got an idea," said Daisy. "Tell Roxy you want *out* of her unusual wedding!"

Rose stared. "Give up the chance to be a flower girl?"

"That's an excellent idea!" said Heather. "This wedding would reflect badly on all the Flower Girls."

"I can't tell Roxy that!" said Violet. "She'd be hurt."

Heather slid close to her on the bench. "Tell Roxy our club rules won't let you be in a punk wedding. Say you're sorry, but a club oath is a club oath."

"We don't have an oath," said Daisy.

Heather tossed her head. "We do now: No punk weddings allowed."

Rose slid close to Violet's other side. "Say you're too shy to do it. You'd be too frightened. Say that you'd get ill. Roxy will understand."

Violet shook her head. "Roxy might. My mother wouldn't. She says it's bad manners to accept an invitation and then change your mind."

Daisy sighed. "Going back on your word *is* rude."

"Roxy's whole wedding is rude! If Violet went back on her word, it would fit the theme," said Heather.

Rose said, "Tell Roxy as nicely as you can, you're sorry."

"Do it, Violet," said Daisy. "You'll be able to sit here with us while Roxy's wedding gets photographed."

Heather pointed across the pond. "Otherwise, you'll be over there with a bouquet of dandelions in your hands."

Violet shivered. She didn't know what to do. She didn't want to let her friends down. She didn't want to let Roxy down.

"There's one other possibility," said Rose.

Violet felt a glimmer of hope. Rose always had good ideas.

"What possibility is that?" asked Daisy.

Rose hesitated. "What if . . ."

She seemed to be thinking hard. "What if Violet didn't try to be a perfect flower girl? What if she went along with Roxy and dressed and acted like the flower girl Roxy wants her to be?"

Violet felt cold all over.

Rose looked pleased and excited. "It would only be for that day. You'd be pretending. Like an actor."

"Violet can't be an actor. She's too shy," said Daisy.

"Violet's too ladylike to dress in anything punk," said Heather.

Rose clenched her fists. Her eyelids fluttered. "Violet is different from you, Heather! She listens to other people. She's different from you, Daisy. She pays attention to what they do and how they talk. She could pretend to be tough. She could imitate Roxy and her friends."

"No, I couldn't." Violet hated to disappoint Rose. But Daisy and Heather were right. She'd have to tell Roxy she couldn't be her flower girl.

Violet got up from the bench. "Thanks, all of you, for trying to help me. I have to go home and get ready for Roxy."

"Stand up for yourself!" called Daisy.

"Don't let her talk you into anything!" called Heather.

As she walked, Violet practiced what she would say to Roxy.

"I can't be your flower girl because . . . Because I'm going to have the measles that day. Because I'm allergic to dandelions. Because I have to do a project for school. . . ."

None of the excuses was very good. Violet knew that. But Roxy was smart. Roxy would get the point.

Violet thought, *She'll see that I don't want to be in her wedding. She'll fling her arms* wide. "Violet," she'll say, "you're a chicken, but I understand."

Violet stopped to fling her own arms wide. In her best Roxy voice she said, "Violet, you're a chicken. . . ."

Violet blinked.

She looked around to make sure no one had heard her.

She'd sounded so much like Roxy, it was frightening.

Chapter 6

"I can't be the kind of flower girl you want," said Violet.

"Pigeon poop," said Roxy.

It was later the same day. Violet and Roxy were sitting in Violet's room on Violet's twin beds.

"I could be a polite kind of flower girl. I could be a pale pink kind of flower girl. But that's all," said Violet.

Roxy glared at Violet. She flopped back on the bed. She folded her arms across her chest. She swung her legs to kick the two rumpled brown paper bags she'd brought instead of a suitcase. "Pigeon poop!" she said again.

Late afternoon sunlight streamed past

the ruffled curtains into the room.

Roxy's diamond nose stud caught the light and flashed.

Violet didn't dare speak.

Roxy sat up.

Her expression had changed. Her eyes were big and pleading. "It's not like you to be selfish, Violet."

Violet thought, *When have I seen her look this way?*

Roxy said, "I've only asked you for the tiniest favor. Your support would mean so much. . . ."

Violet squirmed. "I don't mean to be selfish. I'm telling you the truth. I'm not the right kind of person to be your flower girl. My dress isn't the right kind of dress."

Roxy grasped Violet's hand. She looked deep into her eyes. "This isn't the time to think of yourself. We're talking about my wedding. Won't you even try?"

Violet looked into Roxy's big, pleading eyes. She remembered what Daisy had said. *Roxy could sell anyone anything. . . .*

"Pleeease, Violet?"

Violet couldn't help herself. "I'll do it."

"Great." Roxy stood.

She checked her mascara in Violet's mirror.

She straightened her black leather vest.

Violet had the definite feeling she'd been fooled.

Roxy turned to Violet. She narrowed her eyes. "Next problem: your flower girl dress. Let's see it."

Violet went to the closet. She lifted the garment bag by its satin-covered

55

hanger. She unzipped the bag. Tissue paper rustled. She held up the dress.

Roxy's eyes widened.

She examined the dress from every angle.

She clicked her tongue and shook her head. "Even I would have to act ladylike dressed in this!"

"It's not the dress," said Violet. "It's me."

Roxy took the hanger from Violet. She hung the dress on the closet door. "Don't you believe it! Clothes have power. They're magic. The right piece of clothing can turn you into a girl who's new and strange."

"It can?" said Violet.

Roxy nodded. "Take me, for example. I used to be shy."

Violet blinked. "You were shy? I don't remember that. When?"

Roxy hesitated. "Well, more shy than I am now. Shy compared to my mother."

Roxy pointed to the diamond nose stud. "A friend talked me into getting my nose pierced. That changed everything. I felt like a new woman. As if I were me and . . . more than me."

Violet swallowed hard. Would Roxy try to make her get her nose pierced too?

Roxy said, "Hasn't a piece of clothing ever made you feel like you . . . but something more?"

"More than me?" said Violet.

Roxy sank to a seat on the bed. "Think. There must have been something."

Violet tried to remember. "Mom chooses all my clothes. I feel polite when I wear them. I feel ladylike. I never feel 'more than me.' "

Roxy bent to open one of her brown paper bags. She pulled out three familiar outfits and lay them flat on Violet's bed.

Leopard-skin jumpsuit.

Orange mohair miniskirt and lavender mohair crop top.

White vinyl coat and pink vinyl dress.

Roxy leaned toward Violet. "One of these outfits will make you feel unusual. I guarantee it."

Violet looked from Roxy to the outfits on the bed.

She felt uneasy. She also felt excited. "One of these?"

Roxy drew an *X* across her chest. "Cross my heart and hope to puke. Try one if you don't believe me. See what happens."

Violet hesitated.

Roxy nudged her toward the outfits.

"Choose one. Just try it. Your mother will never know."

Violet chewed her lip.

She stretched out a hand.

Her fingers closed over orange and lavender mohair.

"Put it on," said Roxy.

Violet stepped into the short fuzzy skirt.

She pulled the fuzzy top over her head.

She looked in the mirror. . . .

"*Abracadabra!* You're a strange new girl," said Roxy.

Violet stared.

The girl who gazed back at her looked tough. She looked sure of herself.

Roxy nodded approvingly. "You look *soooo* cool."

Violet couldn't take her eyes off that

59

tough, sure-of-herself girl. She flung her arms wide. "Cool is exactly the way I feel!"

"Violet?" Violet's mother called from downstairs. "Roxy? Dinner is served!"

Violet blinked.

She pulled off the mohair top.

She wriggled out of the mohair skirt. She shot Roxy a worried look. "Let's not tell Mom about this outfit. Not yet."

Chapter 7

Roxy's wedding invitations gave the time of the ceremony: "4 P.M. — more or less."

At two thirty that afternoon, Violet's mother came to her room. She took the pale pink puffed-sleeve dress out of its plastic bag and hung it on the front of Violet's closet door. "Time to get ready," she said.

Violet took a bath.

She dried herself off, sprinkled herself with talcum powder, and combed her wet hair. She put on her bathrobe.

At five past three Rose, Heather, and Daisy arrived. They settled themselves on the guest bed to watch Violet dress.

Violet picked up the new lacy white

underwear her mother had laid out. She put it back in her underwear drawer.

"What are you doing?" said Rose.

Violet picked up the black patent leather Mary Janes her mother had set out. She put them away in her closet.

"Are you going barefoot?" said Heather.

Violet left the pale pink dress hanging where it was. She reached under her bed and dragged out a brown paper bag.

Daisy nudged the others. "Buried treasure!"

Violet opened the paper bag and pulled out the orange mohair miniskirt. She pulled out the lavender mohair crop top. She pulled out orange socks with ruffles and a pair of lavender high-top sneakers. She reached down to the bottom of the bag and pulled out a special present from

Roxy: orange-and-lavender tie-dyed bikini underpants.

She laid everything on her bed.

"They're awful!" said Heather, but she couldn't stop herself from touching them.

"They're beautiful!" said Daisy.

Rose cocked her head. "They're both at the same time."

"Violet, are you ready?" Her mother called from downstairs.

Violet's palms got sweaty.

"Violet?"

She looked in panic at her friends.

"You could stuff the mohair outfit back into the paper bag," said Daisy.

"You could hide the paper bag under your bed," said Rose.

Heather said, "You could put on the white underwear, the Mary Janes, and the pale pink dress. Your mother would never know."

"Do you need help buttoning the buttons, Violet?" called her mother. "Are you having trouble tying the sash? Do you want me to come up and help you?"

"No!" cried Rose, Daisy, and Heather.

Violet shouted, "I don't need help. I'm fine."

She took a step closer to the bed and the orange and lavender mohair outfit. She felt uneasy. She felt excited.

"I'm not going to watch!" Rose covered her eyes but peeked through her fingers.

Daisy silenced her giggles by covering her mouth.

Heather hugged a pillow. "I can't believe you're doing this!"

"Neither can I . . ." Violet slipped off her bathrobe and started to dress.

The clock chimed three thirty. Violet stepped into the living room.

Rose, Daisy, and Heather huddled in the doorway to watch.

"Goodness!" Violet's father peered at

her over his glasses. "I thought you were going to wear pink."

Violet grinned. She flung her arms wide. "I changed my mind."

"What's come over you, Violet?" The horror in Violet's mother's face turned to suspicion. "Did Roxy talk you into this?"

"It was Roxy's idea," Violet admitted. She heard whispered protests behind her.

"But I decided myself."

"Run back upstairs and put on your pale pink dress," said her mother. "You'll look ladylike even if no one else at this wedding does."

In her mohair crop top, Violet felt tough. In her mohair miniskirt, she felt sure of herself. In her high-tops and ruffled socks she was . . . herself but more. "I'll give Roxy back this outfit as soon as the wedding is over," she said. "For now I want to wear it."

"Yay!" Rose, Daisy, and Heather cheered.

Violet's mother turned pale.

"Hurry up, ladies. We're going to be late," said Violet's father.

"It'll just be for a few hours," Violet told her mother. "Then I'll go back to acting ladylike, I promise."

Her mother passed a hand over her eyes. She sighed. "If you promise."

"Yay!" Rose, Daisy, and Heather cheered again.

Violet wanted to cheer, but she didn't. Instead, she straightened her miniskirt and headed for the car.

Chapter 8

Violet's parents drove to the back entrance of Oil City.

They dropped Violet off behind the gas station office, where she was supposed to meet Roxy.

Daisy, Rose, and Heather waved as the car pulled away. They were going around to the front.

Violet stood on the warm pavement and waited.

She looked to the right.

Passersby in cars stared at her crop top.

She looked to the left.

Pedestrians stared at her miniskirt.

Violet crossed her arms to hide her bare midriff.

She began to wish she'd worn the pale pink puffed-sleeve dress. . . .

"*Pssst,* Violet!"

Violet turned.

" 'Here comes the bride!' " Roxy stepped out of the gas station rest room.

"What do you think?" She twirled to show Violet her wedding dress.

Violet caught her breath.

Roxy's ivory-colored dress was cut like a slip. From shoulder to hem it was covered with strands of pearls. They swayed with every move Roxy made.

Roxy repeated, "What do you think?"

"You look beautiful, but . . ." Violet wasn't sure how to answer.

Roxy frowned. "But what?"

Violet had to be honest. "You don't look at all punk."

Roxy laughed and flung her arms

69

wide. The strands of pearly beads moved like liquid. "I'm the bride! I can look any way I want."

Violet laughed too.

"I like this better than a veil." Roxy smoothed her close-fitting cap of pearl beads.

The cap fit like a wig. Strands of pearls lay on Roxy's forehead like long bangs. They fell in a shimmering curtain from the crown of her head to her chin.

"This flapper outfit from the 1920s is my 'something old,'" she said.

Violet marveled. As tough as Roxy acted, underneath she was romantic.

"Here's my 'something borrowed.'" Roxy showed off the black satin, high-heeled pumps she was wearing. They belonged to Violet's mother.

"And my 'something blue.'" Roxy pursed her lips. Her lipstick was purple-blue. It looked glamorous.

Violet ran through the rhyme in her head. *Old, new, borrowed, blue* . . . She looked at Roxy. "Where's your 'something new'?"

"You're it!" Roxy gave Violet's cheek an affectionate pat. "The new, not so well-behaved Violet."

Violet felt embarrassed. She also felt pleased.

Roxy went to peer around the corner of the gas station office. "Come take a look!"

Violet joined her.

The guests had parked their cars side by side to form an aisle between the pumps. Some guests sat inside their cars. Most sat on the hoods or trunks.

"There's Zoot!" Roxy pointed down the aisle of cars.

Zoot wore a black tuxedo jacket and black pants with suspenders.

He looked just like the grooms Violet was used to seeing in Pleasant Park, except for three things. First, none of the other grooms had worn a small, gold hoop earring. Second, none had slashes in the knees of his pants. Third, every Pleasant Park groom wore a stiff white shirt under his tuxedo jacket. Under Zoot's jacket, his chest was completely bare.

"Doesn't he look *nasty*?" Roxy blushed.

Violet spotted her friends. "Look!"

Rose, Daisy, and Heather sat on the hood of Zoot's Hire-a-Heap convertible.

Daisy was giggling. Rose was

straightening her sun hat. Heather was peering down the aisle.

"Ready?" said Roxy.

Violet hitched down the bottoms of her orange-and-lavender tie-dyed bikini underpants. She gripped the dandelion bouquet in both hands. She nodded.

Roxy lifted a bouquet of white long-stemmed roses from the florist's box at her feet. She pulled a giant boom box from the paper bag beside it. "Remember! Don't *walk* down the aisle—strut!"

Violet rehearsed the swaggering stride Roxy had taught her.

Roxy turned the volume to MAX.

She punched the PLAY button.

Music blasted.

She gave Violet a nudge. "Go!"

Violet went.

Violet strutted down the aisle in her

high-tops and ruffled socks. She kept her eye on the spot where Zoot and Father Jake stood.

Some people honked their car horns as Violet passed. Some applauded. Some cheered.

Violet couldn't stop grinning.

"Hey, Little Bo Peep!"

Violet turned to look behind her.

From between two parked cars zoomed the kid on the skateboard. Andre. He whizzed down the aisle toward her. He balanced an ivory satin cushion like a tray on one hand. On the cushion two gold rings gleamed.

Andre circled Violet and gave her an admiring glance. "Verrry cool!"

He slalomed away down the aisle.

Violet smoothed her miniskirt and continued to strut.

 76

Chapter 9

"Everyone look this way!" said the photographer.

Violet stood beside Roxy and Zoot on the grass in Pleasant Park. Over the photographer's shoulder, on the far side of the pond, she could see the bench where she and the other Flower Girls always sat.

This afternoon only three girls sat on the bench. Rose. Daisy. Heather.

The photographer cleared her throat. "That's an awfully polite smile, Violet. Can you look a little less well-behaved?"

"Less well-behaved . . . ?" said Violet.

"Put your hands on your hips," said Roxy.

Violet rested her hands on the orange mohair of her hips.

"Tap one foot," said Roxy.

Violet tapped.

Roxy said, "Now think, 'Don't mess with me!'"

Violet thought it. She narrowed her eyes.

Click! The photographer snapped the picture.

Click! The photographer snapped Violet opening a small gift box while Roxy and Zoot looked on.

"It's for being a good sport," said Roxy.

Violet peered into the box and saw a tiny silver hoop.

"It's a nose ring," said Zoot.

"A snap-on," said Roxy. "For people who don't want to pierce."

Violet attached the ring to her nostril.

Roxy nodded. "It looks like the real thing."

Click!

Click! The photographer snapped Violet standing between her parents.

Violet's snap-on nose ring glowed. Violet stood with her hands on her hips. She tapped her foot and narrowed her eyes.

Violet's mother sighed and raised her eyes heavenward.

Violet's father rested a hand on Violet's lavender mohair shoulder. He smiled as if everything were perfectly normal.

Click! The photographer snapped Violet sitting with Rose, Daisy, and

79

Heather on the hood of Roxy and Zoot's going-away Hire-a-Heap convertible.

Andre skateboarded by. *Click!* She snapped again.

Click! She snapped Rose applying sunblock to Violet's midriff.

Click! Click! She snapped a taxi pulling up to the park and Aunt Glenda stepping out.

Click! Aunt Glenda rushed to kiss Violet's mother.

Click! Aunt Glenda bent to kiss Violet.

Click! Click! Click! She kissed and hugged Roxy again and again. She and Roxy both cried.

Click! Zoot shook hands with Aunt Glenda.

Click! Aunt Glenda hugged and kissed Zoot.

"Hey, Violet!" Zoot caught Violet by the waist and twirled with her over the grass.

Violet gripped Zoot's shoulders. She closed her eyes, tipped back her head, and laughed.

Click! The photographer snapped that too.

Chapter 10

One week later Violet sat with the other Flower Girls on their usual bench in Pleasant Park.

Swans glided on the pond.

Squirrels chattered on the lawn.

The sun shone. A breeze across the pond rustled the gowns of that afternoon's bride and bridesmaids.

A photographer posed the distant party. He snapped.

"I liked your wedding better," Daisy told Violet.

"It was Roxy's wedding, not Violet's," corrected Rose. She tucked a stray lock of hair behind her ear.

For a minute no one said anything.

Rose smiled then. "I liked Violet's wedding better too."

" 'Liked' isn't the way I felt about that wedding." Heather tossed her head. Her cloud of crinkly honey-colored hair bounced. She examined her clear-polished fingernails. "I loathed Roxy's wedding. I hated every tasteless minute of it."

She nudged Violet and grinned. "Let's see the pictures again."

Violet opened the envelope and slid the photos onto her lap.

Daisy pointed. "There's you sashaying down the aisle."

"I wasn't sashaying. I was strutting," said Violet.

"Strutting . . ." Daisy looked at Violet with new respect.

"This one is my favorite." Rose fished a photo from Violet's lap.

It was the one of Zoot twirling Violet over the grass.

Violet remembered the grip of his hands on her waist. She remembered spinning through the air and feeling dizzy, alarmed, and excited, all at the same time.

Violet sighed at the memory. She wondered if she would ever get to feel that way again.

She had given the mohair outfit back to Roxy. Now she wore a starched dress, neatly polished shoes, and not one bit of face jewelry.

Heather studied a photo of Violet and Andre dancing at the reception. They were bumping hips. Heather shook her head. "I saw you with my own eyes, and I still don't believe you acted that way. What came over you, Violet?"

"That orange miniskirt and lavender

crop top came over me," said Violet. She had to tell her friends. "Those clothes were magic!"

"Magic clothes?" Rose tucked a stray lock of hair behind her ear. "Violet, don't be immature."

"But they *were* magic! I put them on and felt like me . . . but more than me. I felt like a strange new girl."

Heather folded her arms. "You're not wearing those clothes now, but you're still acting strange."

"I am?" said Violet.

Heather nodded. "Definitely."

"You're not acting shy or worried," said Daisy.

"You're standing up for yourself," said Rose.

Heather tossed her head. "How do you explain that?"

Violet thought of the orange-and-lavender bikini underpants.

She had kept those.

She was wearing them.

"Speaking of 'magic' clothes," said Daisy. "What happened to your flower girl dress? The pale pink one?"

"My mother stuffed it with tissue paper and put it back in its plastic bag," said Violet.

"She's probably going to return it," said Heather.

Violet shook her head. "Mom is putting it away for safekeeping. She hopes I'll be a normal flower girl someday. In a normal wedding. She hopes I'll wear that dress and act neat, polite . . . ladylike."

"Even a tough kid would act ladylike if she wore that dress," said Daisy.

"Even Roxy would act ladylike!" said Rose.

Violet nodded. "That's what Roxy said when she saw it. If that's not magic, what is?"

"Hey . . ." Daisy blinked. "Maybe with magic clothes, we could be other people too!"

Heather shrugged. "Why would I want to be anyone but me?"

Rose turned to Violet. "What if we wanted to be 'us . . . but more than us?' Do you think we could? Is there a way?"

Violet looked from Daisy to Heather to Rose.

"Well, Violet?" said Rose.

The swans still glided on the pond. The squirrels still chattered on the lawn. But the bridal party across the pond was breaking up. The sun was sinking into the trees.

Violet folded her hands in her lap. She tried to remember how it all had happened. "What changed me wasn't really magic clothes," she said. "Roxy asked me to do her a favor. She asked me not to be selfish. She asked me to try being her kind of flower girl instead of the kind I expected to be. . . ."

"But what's the lesson?" said Rose. "What should we do?"

Violet looked at her three friends. She told them as much as she knew. "If someone ever asks you to be a strange new kind of flower girl . . . don't be nervous. Don't get worried. Say, 'Thank you very much,' and, 'I'd love to. Yes!' "